Over the Rainbow

PERFORMED BY
Judy Collins

MUSIC BY
Harold Arlen

PAINTINGS BY
Eric Puybaret

LYRICS BY
E. Y. Harburg

imagine!
a Peter Yarrow Book
New York
www.imaginebks.com

When all the world is a hopeless jumble
and the raindrops tumble all around,

Heaven

opens a magic lane.

When all the clouds darken up the skyway,

there's a rainbow highway to be found,

Leading from your window pane

to a place behind the sun,

just a step beyond the rain.

Somewhere over the rainbow, way up high,

there's a land that I heard of once in a lullaby.

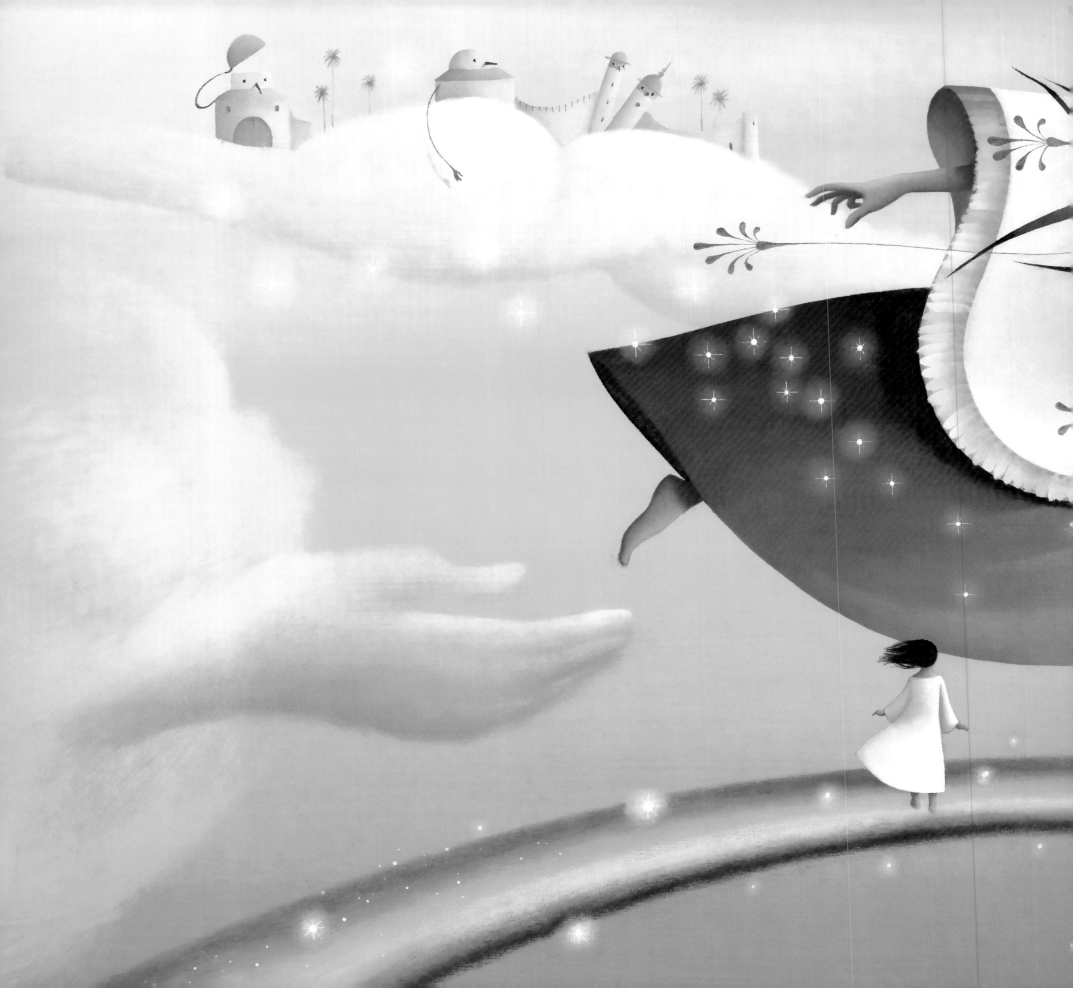

Somewhere over the rainbow skies are blue,
and the dreams that you dare to dream
really do come true.

Some day I'll wish upon a star
and wake up where the clouds
are far behind me.

Where troubles melt like lemon drops,
away above the chimney tops,
that's where you'll find me.

Somewhere over the rainbow,

bluebirds fly.

Birds fly over the rainbow,

why then, oh why can't I?

If happy little bluebirds fly

beyond the rainbow,

Why,
oh, why
can't I?

To my mother, Marjorie, and my father, Chuck, who named me Judy for Judy Garland four months before

"Over the Rainbow" came out on the radio in 1939, with love and gratitude for all you did

to let me fly over my own rainbow. Your loving daughter. ~*Judy*

For Dad and Linette. ~*Eric*

PERFORMER'S NOTE

In the years since I began to play the piano and sing, no song has captured my heart in the way "Over the Rainbow" has. It flies through the years untouched, unblemished, unchanged. It lifts my heart today as it did the first time I heard it. I went to see *The Wizard of Oz* when I was a little girl, with my pigtails tied on top of my head, with my Aunt Betty in Los Angeles. I felt so grown up, and so free, and the song has followed me, like a bluebird, all my life. It is with great pleasure that I sing it here for you, so that you, whatever your age, can feel young and free and hopeful. With Love,

Judy Collins

SINGER, SONGWRITER, AUTHOR, DREAMER

ILLUSTRATOR'S NOTE

In France, my country, "Over the Rainbow" is a well-known song, heard in many versions. I must say that the melody always charmed me, but I never took the time to fully understand the lyrics until I made this book. Over the rainbow–among the magical birds, stars, and clouds–I saw tenderness, hopefulness, reverie, and a little touch of melancholy . . . What an inspiring song!

Eric Puybaret

LIBRARY OF CONGRESS CATALOGING-IN-PUBLICATION DATA

Arlen, Harold, 1905-1986. Over the rainbow / [music by] Harold Arlen ; [lyrics by] E.Y. Harburg ; [paintings by] Eric Puybaret. p. cm.

Summary: Illustrates the well-known song with paintings of a young girl's search for happiness.

ISBN 978-1-936140-00-8

1. Children's songs - United States - Texts. [1. Songs.]
I. Harburg, E. Y. (Edgar Yipsel), 1898-1981. II. Puybaret, Eric, ill. III. Title. PZ8.3.A592Ove 2010
782.42 - dc22 [E] 2009029317

10 9 8 7 6 5 4 3

Published by IMAGINE PUBLISHING, INC.

25 Whitman Road, Morganville, NJ 07751

Music by HAROLD ARLEN

Lyrics by E.Y. HARBURG

© 1938 (Renewed) METRO-GOLDWYN-MAYER INC.

© 1939 (Renewed) EMI FEIST CATALOG INC.

Controlled and Administered by EMI FEIST CATALOG INC. (Publishing)

and ALFRED PUBLISHING CO., INC. (Print)

Illustrations © 2010 ERIC PUYBARET

Printed in China

Manufactured in July 2010

The illustrations in this book were painted using acrylic on linen.

The display type was set in Aphrodite Text & the text type was set in Tonic Book.

Edited by Brooke Dworkin

For information about custom editions, special sales, premium and corporate purchases,

please contact Imagine Publishing, Inc. at specialsales@imaginebks.com